Books by Patricia Reilly Giff you will enjoy:

The Lincoln Lions Band books
illustrated by Emily Arnold McCully

MEET THE LINCOLN LIONS BAND
YANKEE DOODLE DRUMSTICKS
THE "JINGLE BELLS" JAM

The Polka Dot Private Eye books
illustrated by Blanche Sims

THE MYSTERY OF THE BLUE RING
THE RIDDLE OF THE RED PURSE
THE SECRET AT THE POLK STREET SCHOOL
THE POWDER PUFF PUZZLE
THE CASE OF THE COOL-ITCH KID
GARBAGE JUICE FOR BREAKFAST
THE TRAIL OF THE SCREAMING TEENAGER
THE CLUE AT THE ZOO

YEARLING BOOKS are designed especially to entertain and enlighten young people. Patricia Reilly Giff, consultant to this series, received her bachelor's degree from Marymount College and a master's degree in history from St. John's University. She holds a Professional Diploma in Reading and a Doctorate of Humane Letters from Hofstra University. She was a teacher and reading consultant for many years, and is the author of numerous books for young readers.

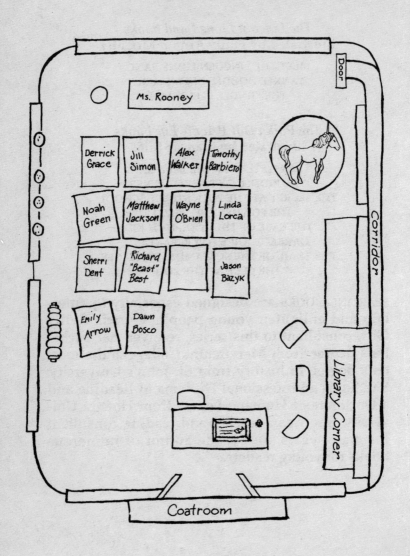

The Kids of the Polk Street School

2.

FISH
FACE

Patricia Reilly Giff

Illustrated by Blanche Sims

A YEARLING BOOK

With love to Laura Cau

Published by
Bantam Doubleday Dell Books for Young Readers
a division of
Bantam Doubleday Dell Publishing Group, Inc.
1540 Broadway
New York, New York 10036

Text copyright © 1984 by Patricia Reilly Giff

Illustrations copyright © 1984 by Blanche Sims

ISBN: 0-440-42557-3

Printed in the United States of America

October 1984

OPM   40   39   38   37   36   35   34   33   32

Chapter 1

"Give me a push, Beast," Emily called to her friend Richard Best.

"I think the bell rang," he said.

She looked over her shoulder. "Just one more little push?"

Beast grabbed the edge of the swing.

He gave her a great push.

Emily sailed up high. She let her head fall back so she could see the sky.

"Everyone's in line," Jill Simon called from the monkey bars.

Emily slid off the swing and landed in a wet patch.

"Yucks," she said. She watched the mud ooze up around her red sneakers.

"We're going to be late," Jill told Emily.

Emily scraped her sneakers against the swing pole. "I'm coming."

1

"It's all right for you," Jill said. "You're the fastest runner in the class. You can catch up."

Emily smiled. She knew she was fast. That was because she had a good-luck charm, her little white rubber unicorn.

"Hey," Beast said. He leaned down over the muddy spot. "Look at this thing go."

"What?" Emily asked.

"A worm. A big fat one."

Emily scrunched down next to him. "He's got a couple of ants on him."

"Ugh," Jill said. "Squish. He's probably full of germs. I'm getting out of here." She started to run for Ms. Rooney's line.

Emily looked after her.

Jill had four braids. Two in front. Two in back. All four of them flapped as she ran.

Beast poked at the worm gently. "I wonder what those ants are doing to him."

"Probably trying to eat him up," Emily said. "Mean."

"Maybe we could save him."

2

Emily nodded. "We can take the ants off. Put him in another spot so they can't find him anymore."

She looked around for a little stick.

"All the kids are inside now," Beast said.

"We'll just have to explain," Emily said. She looked at the big brown doors. "We'll tell Ms. Rooney we had to save this guy's life."

She took a stick and lifted him out of the mud.

"Look how pink he is," Beast said. "And shiny."

"He's a wiggler," Emily said. She watched him curl around the stick.

Beast leaned over and flicked off the ants. "Where should we put him?"

"We've got to find a good muddy place," Emily said. "Worms are crazy about mud."

"How about over there?" Beast said. "Right next to the fence."

Emily held out the stick. She walked slowly so the worm wouldn't drop off. Then she bent over and put him in the mud.

4

They stood there for a minute watching.

"He likes it," Beast said.

"Sure. Wouldn't you? A new home . . . without a pile of ants biting on your back every two minutes."

"I think he's digging a hole," Beast said.

"Good. He'll probably meet up with some other worms."

"Hey, what's that?" Beast asked.

They looked up.

Ms. Rooney was leaning out the window. She clapped her hands. Hard.

"She's clapping at us," Beast said. "Come on."

They started to run.

"Boy, are we in trouble," Emily said when they reached the doors of the Polk Street School. She slapped at her pocket. "Wait a minute. I left my unicorn somewhere."

Beast shook his head. "Ms. Rooney is going to kill us."

"Go ahead," Emily said. "I've got to get him."

5

She dashed across the schoolyard.

The unicorn was right where she had left it—stuck in the swing chain.

She took it out and patted its horn. Then she tucked it in her pocket and started to run.

In the classroom everyone was singing "Oh, Say, Can You See."

Emily tiptoed in.

She opened her mouth and sang loudly.

At the same time she edged her way back to her desk.

After the singing Ms. Rooney said, "Emily Arrow, come up here."

Emily went to the front of the room. She took small steps.

"I'm very disappointed in you," Ms. Rooney said.

"I had to save a worm's life," Emily said.

"Richard saved a worm's life too," Ms. Rooney said, "and he was in five minutes ahead of you."

Emily ducked her head. She looked at her

6

sneakers. They were filthy. She rubbed one of them against the other.

Ms. Rooney sighed. "Take your books. Sit at one of the back desks."

Emily's face felt red. She tiptoed to the back of the room.

She took the desk nearest the radiator. She leaned her arm against the cool metal.

She looked at the backs of all the kids' heads. She could see lots of ears.

Matthew's were the biggest. Alex had little ones, kind of pointy. Jill's were half covered by her braids.

Emily felt her own ears. Regular kind.

She felt all alone back there.

It was going to be a long week.

Chapter 2

On Tuesday Emily made sure she was on time.

She put her lunch in her desk. Then she went over to look at the fishbowl on the science table.

"Hey, Drake," she said. "Look at me."

She tapped her finger on the side of the bowl.

"Hi, Harry."

Harry, the striped one, was twirling around the side of the bowl. Getting exercise, Emily thought.

Drake, the mean one, was gobbling up the food as fast as he could.

He opened his mouth wide.

Then he shut it.

Pop.

Emily opened her mouth a little and popped it shut too.

She dipped her finger into the top of the fish water. It felt wonderful. Cool.

"Time for work," Ms. Rooney said.

Emily dashed back to her desk. She pulled at her new green sweater.

She was hot. Boiling.

She pulled a piece of paper out of her notebook. She folded it back and forth into a fan.

Then she waved it in front of her face.

At the blackboard Ms. Rooney said, "It's a new month. Oc-to-ber." She stretched the word out. "It's a fall month."

"That's because everything is falling," Beast said. He rolled his pencil off his desk.

Everyone laughed.

Even Ms. Rooney.

She wrote a big OCTOBER on the blackboard.

Emily ran her finger under the neck of her sweater. It didn't feel like fall. It felt like summer.

She fanned her neck.

"What's the matter?" Ms. Rooney asked her.

"Nothing." Emily shook her head. She didn't want to say that her sweater was too heavy.

She'd been dying to wear it all week.

It had ribbons on the front and ruffles on the sleeves.

She thought it made her look like that kid on television. The one who had the dog. She couldn't remember her name.

Beast said it made her look like a skinny green string bean.

"October is a happy month," Ms. Rooney said. "We have Columbus Day and Halloween and . . ."

Emily looked out the window. She wished it were winter and snow were falling all over the place.

She'd take off her shoes and jump in the biggest pile of snow she could find.

She'd stamp in it.

Her feet would turn icy cold and purple.

Just then the classroom door opened. It was the principal, Mr. Mancina. There was a girl with him.

She had curly brown hair and little red ladybug earrings.

Emily pushed at her own straight-as-a-stick hair. She flicked at her ears.

No earrings.

Plain.

Her mother said she couldn't have her ears pierced until she was ten. At least.

Maybe she should ask again. Beg.

"We have a new girl," Mr. Mancina said. "Here from Florida."

Emily thought about waving to the new girl. She wondered if the new girl would think it was funny that Emily was sitting at the back desk.

Emily was glad she had on her new sweater, even though it was hot as a furnace.

"This is Dawn," Mr. Mancina said. "Dawn Bosco."

Ms. Rooney said, "Let's find a seat for you, Dawn."

"Over here," yelled Matthew.

Emily raised her hand. Dawn would be sorry if she had to sit near Matthew's desk.

Matthew was a good kid.

But he still wet the bed. You had to try not to breathe when you sat near him.

Ms. Rooney looked at Emily and nodded. "Sit next to Emily," she told Dawn.

Emily looked up at Ms. Rooney.

She was the best teacher in the whole school.

She was probably the best teacher in the whole world, Emily thought.

Dawn came down the aisle. She slid into the desk next to Emily.

While Ms. Rooney talked with Mr. Mancina, Dawn began to unpack her schoolbag. She pushed Emily's notebook a little so it wasn't on her desk.

"You have a pretty name," Emily whispered to her.

Dawn didn't say anything. She took a notebook out of her schoolbag. It was pink with flowers on it.

Then she unpacked her pencil box. It was the kind with drawers. Inside were paper clips. And erasers. And little round things to stick on looseleaf.

It had everything. Even a blue pencil with a pink tassel.

At last Dawn looked at her. "What's your name again?"

"Emily."

"Oh," Dawn said.

Emily waited for Dawn to say that she had a pretty name too.

Instead, Dawn said, "My middle name is Tiffanie."

Lucky.

"That's nice," Emily said. She tried to pull the edge of her sweater away from her stomach without letting Dawn see.

"What's your middle name?" Dawn asked.

Emily didn't answer at first. She didn't have a middle name.

Dawn began again. "What's—"

"Theresa," Emily said. "Emily Theresa Arrow."

Dawn flicked the tassel on her pencil.

Emily wished she had told Dawn that her name was Carmelita. Or Millicent.

Beast turned around and smiled.

"Who's that?" Dawn asked.

"Beast."

"Where did he get that crazy name?"

Emily raised her shoulders. "His last name is Best. Beast for Best."

Dawn made a little face.

"We have fish," Emily said. "Wayne brought them in for the science table. Harry and Drake. Drake makes faces."

She opened her mouth as wide as she could.

Then she snapped it shut.

Pop.

Dawn looked back at the fish. "We have a gerbil in my old school. A big one."

Emily reached into her desk and pulled out her unicorn. She rubbed its long dainty horn. "I take him all over the place," she told Dawn. "Even to bed. He sleeps on my pillow."

Emily clicked her tongue. She galloped the unicorn across her desk.

"Can I see?" Dawn held out her hand.

Emily thought for a second. Then she gave him to Dawn.

Dawn danced him up and down on her arm.

"Good-bye," Mr. Mancina told the children. "Have a good day." He closed the door behind him.

"Now," said Ms. Rooney. "Back to work." She shook her head. "Where were we?"

"October," Jill called out.

"Oh, yes," Ms. Rooney said. "Fall. And Columbus." She laughed. "It's even my birthday month. October seventh."

Emily looked up at Ms. Rooney. She wondered how old she was.

Maybe the class could give her a surprise birthday party. The fourth-graders had given Mrs. Kerwin one last week.

She counted on her fingers. Today was the first. Wednesday was the second. She closed her eyes. Thursday. Friday. Saturday. Sunday.

Monday. Ms. Rooney's birthday was next Monday.

16

Ms. Rooney was right. October was going to be a great month.

She turned to Dawn.

The unicorn wasn't on the desk.

"Where's Uni?" she asked.

Dawn frowned. "I gave him to you a minute ago."

"No. I—"

"Look in your desk."

"Girls," Ms. Rooney said. She put her finger on her lips. "It's time for gym."

Chapter 3

That day gym was outside in the schoolyard.

Everyone raced down the stairs and out the big brown doors.

Emily was right behind Dawn. "Hey," she said. "I want my unicorn."

Dawn shook her head. "I told you. I gave him back. You weren't paying any attention."

"Are you sure?" Emily asked. She wished she had taken time to look in her desk. As soon as they got back in the classroom she'd—

"Cross my heart," Dawn said. "Spit on my big toes."

Just then Mr. Bell, the gym teacher, blew his whistle.

"Today we'll have races," he said. "We'll see who the best runners are."

Richard turned around. "That's you, Emily," he said. "You're really fast."

Dawn looked at Emily. "I'm really fast too."

"Matthew's fast too," Alex said. "He's as fast as a . . . as a . . ."

"Racing car," Matthew yelled. He sped around them. "Vroom. Vroom."

"Boy," Dawn whispered. She was looking at Matthew. "Does that kid smell!"

"Shh," Emily said. She hoped Matthew hadn't heard.

But Matthew's head was down. His face was red.

"Alex is right," Emily said. "You're the best, Matthew."

"Not as fast as you, Emily," Matthew said. He kicked at a pebble with his sneaker.

"Pay attention," Mr. Bell said. He pointed. "This is going to be a long race. Down the school-yard to the end. Touch the tree. Then back again."

Emily patted her pocket. She wished she had her unicorn. He gave her good luck.

She pulled at her sweater. She wished she had a glass of water. A glass with ice cubes piled high.

19

Dawn touched one of the ribbons on her sleeve. "That's a nice sweater," she said. "I have one with ribbons too. Pink. I like pink a little better than green, I think. Don't you?"

"Line up," Mr. Bell said.

All the kids made a line.

Emily hoped Matthew would come in first.

Poor Matthew.

"Ready," Mr. Bell yelled.

Everyone crouched down. Emily dusted off her sneakers.

"Get set," yelled Mr. Bell.

Emily took a deep breath. Out of the corner of her eye she could see Dawn. Dawn didn't have sneakers on. She was wearing shiny black shoes.

Dawn edged up a little bit. Her feet were right at the line in the cement. Emily edged her feet up too.

"Go," shouted Mr. Bell.

Emily started to run. She took big flying steps.

She passed everyone. Jill and Beast. Dawn. Matthew.

Emily loved to run. She always held her unicorn. She made believe she was the unicorn. Her long horn pointed forward. Her mane flew in the wind.

Today was different. Without the unicorn she felt slow. She could hear Matthew coming up behind her. Passing her.

Matthew was at the tree now. He touched it and started back.

Emily tried to run faster. She reached the tree and touched it with her fingertips.

Then she turned. She felt as if she couldn't make her feet move fast enough. Without the unicorn she was just an ordinary runner. Not fast. Not special.

Suddenly she could see Dawn out of the corner of her eye.

Close.

Emily's sweater rubbed under her arms.

It was too hot. Itchy.

She could hardly catch her breath.

Then Dawn was next to her.

Matthew dashed across the finish line. "Come on, Emily," he yelled.

But it was too late.

Dawn threw herself forward.

"The new girl," Mr. Bell yelled. "Second. Terrific running.

"Third. Emily Arrow.

"Fourth. Richard Best."

Jill was crying.

Jill always cried when she didn't win.

Emily patted her on the back. She knew how Jill felt.

Then she sank down to lean against the wall of the school. She lifted the back of her sweater a little so she could feel the bricks.

They were rough. Cool.

Dawn sat down next to her.

"That was good," Emily said, even though she didn't want to.

Dawn smiled. "I know. You should see me

with my sneakers on. My good ones. No one can catch me then. Not even that kid Matthew.''

Emily scratched at her back. She wanted to say "You should see me when I have my unicorn.'' But she didn't say anything.

She wished Dawn weren't sitting next to her. She wished Dawn were in her old school.

She wished she were alone at the back desks again, just looking at everybody's ears.

Chapter 4

Emily was the first one back in the classroom.

She raced down the aisle. She pulled everything out of her desk.

Her pencils. *Moving On*, her reader. A yellow leaf she had made in art.

The unicorn wasn't there.

"See," she said to Dawn. "I told you. You didn't give Uni back."

Emily opened her eyes wide. She didn't want the new girl to think she was ready to cry.

"I did so," Dawn said.

"Give him back," Emily said.

"You look like a fish," Dawn said. "You look just like those fish in the back of the room. Harry and what's his name."

Emily stuck her face up right next to Dawn's.

She opened her mouth wide.

As wide as she could.

25

Then she snapped it shut.

Pop.

Dawn jumped back. "Fish face," she said.

"You're not coming to the party," Emily said.

Dawn began to cry.

Ms. Rooney stopped watering her begonia plant. "What's going on in here?" she asked.

Everyone in the class was watching them. They looked as if they felt sorry for the new girl.

Nobody knew that she was horrible, Emily thought.

Nobody knew that she had taken Uni.

"Emily Arrow is scaring me," Dawn told Ms. Rooney. "She said I can't go to her party."

Ms. Rooney frowned. "Emily, I thought your birthday was in July."

Emily put her head down.

"Well?" Ms. Rooney asked.

"July fourth," Emily said in a low voice.

"See then," Ms. Rooney said to Dawn. "You don't have to worry. By next summer you and Emily will be friends again. Stop crying."

"She took my unicorn," Emily said. "My lucky unicorn."

Ms. Rooney raised her eyebrows. "Dawn . . ."

"I gave it back," Dawn said.

Ms. Rooney looked at Emily.

Emily shook her head. "It wasn't there."

"Let's all look in our desks," Ms. Rooney said. "This is a good chance to clean everything out."

In front of her Beast began to pile stuff on top of his desk.

Beast was a great artist. He kept drawing a million pictures.

Everything always landed inside his desk.

It was a mess.

Up in the front Jill was cleaning out her desk. Jill was so neat, there was almost nothing inside her drawer.

Everyone was talking.

Books were dropping all over the place.

Matthew found a Fluffernutter sandwich he had forgotten to eat.

27

People kept running up to the front of the room with their junk. The wastebasket was piled high with old workbook pages.

Ms. Rooney even looked in the closet.

But nobody found Uni.

"I'm sorry, Emily," Ms. Rooney said. "I know you loved that unicorn."

Emily felt a big lump in her throat.

She'd never see the unicorn again.

She looked at Dawn out of the corner of her eye.

Dawn wasn't crying anymore.

She was playing with her pencil box.

Emily leaned over. "My father is a cop, you know."

Dawn didn't say anything.

"I might ask him to come to school. He can check people's fingerprints."

Dawn put her pencil box in her desk. "Fish face," she whispered.

Emily opened and shut her mouth a couple of

times. She made a nice fat popping sound. "You're still not coming to the party."

Dawn raised her hand.

"Put your hand down, Dawn," Ms. Rooney said. "It's time to do our spelling."

Emily spent a few minutes picking at a little peel of paint on the radiator. Then she pulled out her notebook.

She wrote her words as fast as she could.

Then she tore a new paper out of her notebook.

She wet her pencil a little. It really needed sharpening, but it was too late for today.

Ms. Rooney wouldn't let anybody sharpen after the Pledge anymore. That was because Alex sharpened his pencil twelve times the other day. By the afternoon his pencil was a little teeny thing. And Ms. Rooney said he had wasted the whole day.

Emily smoothed out her paper.

Dear Class, she wrote in her best handwriting.

Then she thought some more.

She wanted to say Let's give Ms. Rooney a surprise party.

But she didn't know how to spell all that.

Besides, Ms. Rooney might see the paper when she passed it around.

Ms. Rooney always saw everything.

Emily crumpled up the paper.

It was time for reading help. Emily followed Beast and Matthew and Alex out of the classroom and down the hall to Room 100.

Mrs. Paris was waiting for them.

"Next Monday is Ms. Rooney's birthday," Emily said.

"Nice," Mrs. Paris said. "Birthdays are fun."

"Maybe we can give her a party," Emily said. "A surprise party."

"That's a lovely idea," Mrs. Paris said.

"I'll make some pictures for her," Beast said.

"We can hang them up," Emily said. "And get crepe paper."

"And balloons," Matthew said. "Red ones."

"My mother will let me make a cake," Emily said.

"Chocolate, I hope," said Alex.

"Good," Mrs. Paris said. "I'll help you. If you get all these things, we'll decorate the classroom early Monday morning, before Ms. Rooney gets to school."

Emily nodded. She'd tell the rest of the kids at lunchtime. All of them except Dawn Tiffanie Bosco.

Chapter 5

Emily hurried down the hall. She tried not to think about how sleepy she was. Without Uni on her pillow last night it took a long time to get to sleep.

Today was Wednesday. She loved Wednesday.

Hot dogs for hot lunch. Chocolate pudding for dessert.

And right after lunch Ms. Rooney's class had art.

Emily stopped at the classroom door.

There was another teacher sitting at Ms. Rooney's desk.

A substitute teacher.

It was the one with the fat stomach and the little skinny legs.

The one who yelled all the time.

Wednesday was ruined.

Slowly Emily walked into the classroom. She said hi to Beast and Jill and waved at Matthew.

Dawn was there already, fooling around with her pencil box.

She said hello as Emily slid into her seat.

Emily didn't answer her.

"You're just mad because I can run faster than you can," Dawn said.

"That's not true," Emily said, even though she knew it was a little true.

Emily looked over at the radiator.

There was a little sign taped to the side. It said STOP PICKING PAINT.

It was signed JIM.

He was the man who cleaned up.

Emily stared at the radiator. She had picked off a big piece yesterday. It looked like a picture of an ugly girl. A girl with curly hair. It looked like Dawn Tiffanie Bosco.

Emily began to copy her boardwork. It was a story about Christopher Columbus.

She wished he had a shorter name.

The whole story had a lot of hard words.

Maybe she should ask Dawn again about the unicorn.

Ask her nicely.

Tell her that she really loved the unicorn.

Tell her that—

"Last call for hot lunch," the substitute teacher said.

Emily rushed up to the front.

She put her money on the teacher's desk. One of the dimes rolled off the desk onto the floor.

When that happened, Ms. Rooney always laughed. "Are you trying to throw your money away, Emily?" she would say.

But this teacher didn't laugh. She didn't even smile. "Pay attention," she said.

Emily dived for the dime. She put it carefully on the desk. "Two desserts, please," she said. She tried to remember the teacher's name.

"All that chocolate isn't good for you," the teacher said, but she tore off two blue dessert tickets anyway.

Emily went back to her desk. She hoped that Ms. Rooney would be back by tomorrow.

Emily looked over at Dawn's paper. She had finished her Christopher Columbus story already.

It was beautiful.

No cross-outs.

No erasings.

Emily looked at her own Christopher Columbus paper.

It was a mess. She saw that she had copied the same thing twice. *Christopher Columbus sailed the ocean sailed the ocean. He was very brave.*

Dawn would probably turn out to be the smartest kid in the whole class.

And the best runner.

With the best pencil box.

And she had Uni too.

Emily felt a hard lump in her throat.

She crumpled up her paper into a tiny ball.

She walked up to the wastebasket with it.

The substitute teacher looked up. She frowned.

"You'd better get down to business," she told Emily in a loud voice.

Suddenly the teacher's name popped into Emily's head. Mrs. Miller.

Miller the killer, she told herself.

She couldn't wait to tell Beast the poem she had just made up.

Miller the killer.

Maybe she could add to it. Miller the killer is a diller. Miller the killer is—

Hey, Emily thought. Miller the killer is a gorilla.

Emily started to laugh. Quickly she covered her mouth.

She took out a new piece of paper. In her neatest handwriting she began to copy *Christopher* . . .

Miller the killer is a gorilla.

She could feel the laughing in her throat and in her stomach.

It wouldn't stop.

She pressed her lips together.

The laughing exploded out through her nose.

Mrs. Miller looked up again. "Who's that?"

Emily ducked her head. She looked at the picture of the ugly girl on the radiator. The Dawn Tiffanie girl.

Mrs. Miller got up from the desk.

Mrs. Miller the gorilla.

Emily bit her lip. She could feel her shoulders shaking. "Stop," she said to herself. "Stop."

"I see you," Mrs. Miller said to Emily. "If you think I'm going to put up with your nonsense all day, young lady, you're mistaken."

Emily felt her face get hot.

"Pick up your notebook," Mrs. Miller said, "and sit outside in the hall."

"I'll stop," said Emily. Only the really bad kids sat outside in the hall.

"You heard me," Mrs. Miller said. "Write your spelling words ten times each. Sit right outside the door."

Anyone who saw her out there would know that she was a bad kid.

And lots of people walked down that hall. Mrs.

Paris, the reading teacher; Mrs. Ames, the nurse. Sixth-graders. Sometimes even Mr. Mancina, the principal.

Emily could see the whole class was watching her.

Everyone felt sorry for her.

She picked up her notebook. She put her head up in the air so nobody would think she was going to cry.

She walked out the classroom door.

Everything was going wrong since the unicorn was gone.

She slid down against the hall wall and sat on the floor.

Chapter 6

Nobody else was out in the hall.

Emily opened her speller. She counted.

There were fifteen spelling words this week.

Fifteen words ten times each.

She couldn't even begin to count how many words that was.

It would probably take her all day.

She folded her paper into four columns.

The first word was chin.

She made a line of *c*'s down the page.

Next to it she made a line of *h*'s.

Then she wrote ten *in*'s.

"Chin," she mumbled to herself.

The door opened.

It was Beast.

He slid down on the floor next to her.

"What are you doing here?" she asked. She smiled. It was good to have company.

"Chewing gum," Beast said. "I forgot to take it out of my mouth when I got to school this morning." He stopped to feel his teeth.

"Your front teeth are coming in pretty good," Emily said. She looked at the two new curly teeth Richard was growing. One was longer than the other.

It looked terrible, Emily thought.

"Going to be nice and big," Richard said. He ran his finger over the longer one.

Emily reached into her pocket for a ball-point pen. She started to paint her fingernails with it. It took a long time. After she finished her thumb and her pinkie, she looked up. "Do you have to write your spelling words?"

Beast nodded. "Five times."

"Five times? I wonder why I have to do it ten times." She held her nails out.

"Don't worry," Beast said. "I write slow. I'll stay out here with you until you're all finished."

Emily sighed. "I hope Ms. Rooney comes back

soon. I hope she comes back in time for her party."

"So do I," Beast said. He started to write.

She leaned over his shoulder. "You're spelling chin wrong."

Beast scratched out a bunch of *Chine*'s.

"My mother said she'd make a cake with me," Emily said. "A big one with gumdrops on top of it."

"I don't like gumdrops," Beast said. "But that's all right. I'll eat the rest of it."

"I don't like that new girl," Emily said. "I think she took Uni, my unicorn."

Beast looked up.

"I couldn't run fast yesterday without Uni. I couldn't go to sleep last night. I got in trouble today. All because of Dawn Tiffanie Bosco."

"That's terrible," Beast said. He thought for a moment. "Do you think Mrs. Miller will let us go to recess this morning?"

Emily shook her head.

"You think she'll just leave us here?"

"Maybe."

"We could look in Dawn's desk," Beast said.

Emily nodded her head slowly. "That's a good idea, Beast," she said. "A great idea."

They stopped talking while Mrs. Avery, the music teacher, passed.

Emily tried to hide her face a little so Mrs. Avery wouldn't see who it was.

After Mrs. Avery turned the corner, Emily said, "I'm sick of sitting here. I'd like to get up and—" She tried to think of something interesting. "Get up and run around the school as fast as I can."

"Go ahead," Richard said.

"Suppose Mrs. Miller comes out? Mrs. Miller, the killer, the gorilla."

"Hey, that's good," Richard said.

"That's what I was laughing at."

Richard started to laugh. "Mrs. Gorilla the killer is a ziller."

The door opened. It was Jill. This morning she was wearing blue ribbons on all her braids.

"Mrs. Miller said you can come in now," Jill said. "She's going to give you one more chance."

Emily looked at Beast.

"That's because I begged her," Jill said.

"Too bad," Beast said. "Things were just starting to be fun out here."

They picked up their books and followed Jill back into the classroom.

"Don't worry," Beast whispered. "We'll look through Dawn's desk at recess."

That day recess wasn't until eleven o'clock.

By then it had started to rain. Hard.

Mrs. Miller looked out the window. "Too bad," she said.

Too bad, Emily thought too. She was dying to see if her unicorn was in Dawn Tiffanie Bosco's desk.

It would have to wait until the next day.

Chapter 7

It was Thursday.

Emily was certainly glad that Wednesday was over. There had been a change in the lunch. No two chocolate puddings for dessert.

Instead, there had been peaches. Slimy ones with syrup.

The monitor had made her eat two bowls of them.

And no art in the afternoon.

But today was going to be a good day. Even though Miller Ziller was there again, sitting at Ms. Rooney's desk.

Today was the day she'd get Uni back.

In front of her Beast was bent over his desk. Emily sat up tall so she could see what he was doing.

She knelt up on her chair.

Beast turned around and saw her looking. He held the picture up.

He was drawing a girl and a boy. They looked as if they were sneaking around.

Emily felt her heart begin to beat a little faster.

She knew what he was drawing. He was drawing himself. And her. They were sneaking into the classroom to search through Dawn's desk.

She hoped they wouldn't be caught.

Right then Dawn was reading her reader. She was way past the rest of her group.

It looked as if she were going to finish the whole reader today. All by herself.

Ms. Rooney was going to be mad as anything, Emily thought. Everybody was supposed to stay right with his group.

That Dawn was a show-off.

Emily wished she could read a whole reader in three days. Especially a big fat one.

Dawn looked over at her. "You have blue nail polish?" She looked as if she wished she had blue nail polish too.

"Expensive," Emily said.

"Where did you get it?"

Emily looked up at the ceiling. She tried to think of what to say. "My sister gave it to me. Stacy."

It was really true. Stacy had found the ballpoint pen on the floor in the living room behind the television.

"How old is she?" Dawn asked.

Emily made believe she didn't hear Dawn. She didn't want to say that Stacy was only four and a quarter.

It was time for boardwork. It was examples. Add and take away. A whole bunch of them. Easy.

Emily did them in about four minutes.

Next to her Dawn was still working on take-aways. She made a line of sticks on her paper. A big long line. Then she crossed most of them out. At the same time she was counting out loud.

It sounded as if she were doing it all wrong.

Dawn saw her and quickly covered her paper.

Then she turned it over and put her hand on top of it.

Emily grinned to herself.

At least there was one thing Dawn Tiffanie Bosco couldn't do.

Recess time was in the afternoon. Emily thought it would never come. At last Mrs. Miller made them line up.

Emily and Beast were the last two out of the classroom.

When the line turned the corner, Emily and Beast stood still.

Emily bent over the water faucet and took a long drink.

The water was warm. It tasted like broccoli. Rusty. It left a taste in her mouth.

"Come on," Beast said.

They ducked back down the hall and into the classroom.

It was a mess.

Ms. Rooney always made them take everything off their desks when they went out of the room.

But Mrs. Miller didn't care.

"Come on over here," Beast said.

Emily went over to the window.

She could see the schoolyard. At one end the third-graders were playing ball.

Then Mrs. Miller and the rest of the second-grade class appeared.

She watched as Mrs. Miller blew her whistle. She was waving her arms around.

The second-graders made a circle.

"She's going to play that same babyish game as last time," Richard said. "Who's Got the Flag?"

"I think she made it up by herself," Emily said. "I bet the kids are mad."

"Go ahead," Beast said. "Get your unicorn."

Emily looked at him. "I don't think this is right," she said. "I feel funny."

Beast sat on the edge of Matthew's desk. "It's not right that she has your unicorn."

Slowly Emily went back to Dawn's desk.

She pulled out a book and a piece of paper.

"Anything else in there?" Richard asked.

51

"Her pencil box, I think."

With one finger Emily touched the little knob on the pencil box drawer. Slowly she pulled it open.

She could see the dainty white horn, the little legs.

"Beast," she whispered. "He's here."

"What are you doing in this room?" a voice said.

Emily jumped.

It was Mrs. Kettle, the strictest teacher in the whole school.

Emily felt her face get hot.

Dawn's paper fluttered to the floor.

"What are you doing here?" Mrs. Kettle asked again.

Emily looked at Beast. Her heart was pounding. Richard looked as if his heart were pounding too. He slid off Matthew's desk.

"We came back because—" Emily began.

Mrs. Kettle put her hand up. There was a big frown right in the middle of her forehead. "Never

mind," she said. "Just go where you're supposed to go."

Emily reached for the pencil box.

"Just your book," Mrs. Kettle said impatiently. "And go."

"But . . ." Emily began.

"Come on, Emily," Beast said.

Emily tucked Dawn's reader under her arm.

"And pick up that paper you just dropped," Mrs. Kettle said. "This room is a mess. Wait until Ms. Rooney comes back and sees it."

Emily bent down and picked up the paper. Then she followed Beast to the front of the room and out the door.

Outside in the hall Emily looked back.

Mrs. Kettle was still standing there in the doorway. Her hands were on her hips.

Emily and Beast rushed around the corner and started down the stairs.

"We nearly got killed," Beast said. "Do you know that?"

"I know it," Emily said. "I thought she was

going to take us to Mr. Mancina." She took a deep breath. "Beast, she has Uni."

"Don't worry," Beast said. "We'll get him back. We'll tell Mrs. Miller when we get back in the classroom."

Emily nodded. "What are we going to do about this stuff?" She held out Dawn's reader and the paper.

"Is that her homework?" Beast asked.

Emily looked down at the paper.

" 'Dear Karen,' " she read aloud. "No. I think it's a letter."

"Stick it inside the book," Beast said.

"Then what?"

"Good question." Beast scratched the side of his ear. "Maybe we should go back to the classroom and—"

"I don't think so," Emily said. She stopped on the bottom step. "Beast, listen."

"I wrote a letter once," Beast said. "It was hard. I couldn't spell any of the words."

Emily read aloud.

"Dear Karen,

I hate this school. There are no friends. I did a bad thing. It was terrible.

I hate Amlee. She is mean. She makes fish faces.

I miss you.

XXXXXXXXXX

Dawn"

"A bad thing," Emily said. "She certainly did."

"She must be crazy," Beast said. "I don't even know what a fish face is."

Emily opened her mouth wide.

Then she snapped it shut. Pop.

"You look like Harry," Beast said.

"No. Drake."

Beast grinned. "Who's Amlee? We don't have an Amlee here."

Up above them Mrs. Kettle leaned over the stair rail. "If you two don't go where you belong, I'm going to take you straight to Mr. Mancina's office."

Emily and Beast didn't answer. They rushed to the big doors.

Outside they ducked behind the side of the school. "I'm Amlee," Emily said.

"Are you mean?"

"Of course not," Emily said.

Beast pointed. "The class is lining up."

"We'll wait here," Emily said. "We'll get on the end of the line when they go by."

She leaned back against the bricks.

If only she could get the unicorn back. She missed it on her pillow every night. She missed it in her pocket every day.

Suddenly Emily thought about the book under her arm.

"Hey, Beast," she said. "What about Dawn's book?"

Beast took a breath. "I forgot," he said.

"Hurry. Think," Emily said. "Here they come."

Beast raised his shoulders up in the air. "Maybe she won't know it's hers. Maybe you can put it back when we get upstairs."

57

She and Beast ducked back as Mrs. Miller and the class marched by.

Then they slipped in behind them.

Emily made sure that Dawn was way ahead of her.

When she reached the classroom, she slid the book on top of the bookcase at the side of the room. Dawn would be sure to see it any minute. She'd never guess that Emily had put it there.

Emily sat down next to Dawn. "I want my unicorn," she said.

Dawn looked down at the desk. "I don't have it."

Emily raised her hand. She waved it in the air.

Mrs. Miller shook her head. "Don't bother me now. It's time to go home."

Everyone lined up.

"My father's going to arrest you," Emily told Dawn at the door.

For a minute Dawn looked scared. Then she raced down the hall.

Jill Simon was standing behind Emily. She followed her outside. "Your father's going to put Dawn in jail?" she asked. She looked worried.

Emily shook her head. "No." She was sorry Jill had heard. "Don't tell anyone I said that. My father wouldn't like it if he found out."

"I won't," Jill said. She sucked on the edge of her braid. "Dawn was crying in the bathroom, I think."

"Dawn's a baby," Emily said.

"I think she wants someone to be friends with," Jill said. She took her braid out of her mouth. It was a little wet on the end. "Dawn said she'd teach me how to do double Dutch jump rope. She said she'd show you too."

Emily twitched her shoulder. She didn't want Jill to know that she wished she could learn how to do double Dutch jump rope.

"She said we could learn it in two minutes," Jill said. "She said we could come over to her house someday."

Emily thought about learning double Dutch. Then she thought about her unicorn. "I don't think Dawn wants to make friends," she said. "I don't think she cares about anything."

Chapter 8

It was Friday. A plain day. No gym. No music. No anything.

Hot lunch was melted cheese sandwiches. They were always burned around the edges. And sticky.

Emily felt horrible.

She had watched Dawn come in that morning. She didn't have her pencil box with her.

Now they couldn't even tell Mrs. Miller.

Dawn still hadn't found her book.

She was looking all over the place.

Emily could see it. It was sitting right there on top of the bookcase, just waiting for Dawn to spot it.

But Dawn kept looking in her desk.

When Emily said, "What's the matter?" Dawn didn't even answer her.

Dawn was a mean one, all right, Emily thought.

Emily picked one little piece of the radiator paint.

The radiator girl looked uglier than ever.

Emily twisted her head to get a better look. The radiator girl didn't have curly-looking hair anymore. She had straight hair.

She looked like Emily. Emily Arrow.

Silly, Emily thought. She did not.

She wished Dawn would find her reader.

She wished she hadn't read Dawn's letter.

Emily hoped she'd never meet Dawn's friend. Dawn's friend would think she was the mean one.

If she could spell better, she'd write a letter to Dawn's friend too. She'd tell her that Dawn was a stealing kind. Stealing people's unicorns.

That day reading groups were in the afternoon.

Mrs. Miller called the middle group first.

Dawn was still looking for her reader.

Mrs. Paris, the reading teacher, stuck her head in the door. She waved at Emily. ''No reading today,'' she said. ''I have to go to a meeting.''

''That's all right,'' Mrs. Miller said.

Ugh, Emily thought. Mrs. Miller would read

with Emily's group instead. She'd make them clap for sounds.

Emily could never do that right.

Plop. A note landed on her desk. Jill turned around and smiled at her.

Emily read the note.

> E.
>
> My mother said I can bring some candy for the party.
>
> J.

Emily smiled back at Jill. Next to her Dawn was banging books on top of her desk.

Emily thought about the party. She wondered what Dawn would think on Monday when she saw the classroom all fixed up for the party.

Emily wondered how she'd feel.

Maybe she'd feel horrible.

Just the way Emily felt right then.

"Where's your pencil box?" Emily asked.

Dawn's face got red. "I left it home."

"What's the matter?" Emily asked. "Are you looking for something?"

"I lost my book," Dawn said. She looked as if she were going to cry. "I have to find it before Mrs. Miller calls my group."

"Maybe it's not in your desk," Emily said slowly. "Maybe it's somewhere else in the room."

Dawn shook her head. "It was right here."

"Oh," Emily said. She could hear Mrs. Miller making the middle group clap for sounds.

"Pancake," Mrs. Miller said.

Clap, clap went the middle group.

"Good," said Mrs. Miller. "Try this one. Place."

The middle group clapped once.

"Maybe it fell out of your desk," Emily said.

Dawn shook her head.

"Maybe someone borrowed it," Emily said slowly.

"Maybe someone stole it," Dawn said. Then she shook her head again. "I guess no one would steal my reader."

"I guess not," Emily said. She looked at the bookcase. It wasn't as easy to see the book as she had thought it was.

Maybe she should go to the bathroom. She'd have to pass right by the bookcase. She'd give the book a little push. Then Dawn would be sure to see it.

She stood up.

Mrs. Miller looked at her. "All right," she said. "Emily's group may come to read with me now."

Slowly Emily went to the reading table.

Mrs. Miller smiled at them. "Today we're going to clap for sounds," she said. "Won't that be fun?"

Emily sighed. She kept thinking about Dawn.

She didn't know why she felt so bad about Dawn's reader. After all, Dawn had stolen her unicorn.

"What's the matter with you, Emily?" Mrs. Miller asked. "Why aren't you clapping with the rest of the group? You'd better do a few words by yourself.''

Emily swallowed. Out of the corner of her eye she saw Dawn watching her.

Emily looked at Mrs. Miller. Mrs. Miller was trying to think of a word. She was probably thinking of the hardest word in the second grade for Emily to clap.

"Try this one, Emily," Mrs. Miller said. "Wish."

Emily clapped once.

She was glad when Mrs. Miller nodded. She looked over at Dawn.

Dawn was still watching.

"Spider," Mrs. Miller said.

Emily closed her eyes. Sp, i, der, she thought. One, two, three.

Emily clapped three times.

Dawn shook her head.

"Two, I mean," Emily said. "Spi-der."

"Good," said Mrs. Miller.

Emily looked at Dawn. She wondered why she had helped her.

Dawn smiled a little.

Mrs. Miller looked at her watch. "No time for the top group. It's almost time to go home."

Emily went back to her desk. She packed her books. Dawn had given up looking for her reader.

All of Dawn's books were packed. When the bell rang, she was the first one in the line.

Emily grabbed her books. She went up to Dawn. She wanted to say, "Bring your pencil box on Monday. Bring my unicorn." Instead, she looked at Dawn for a moment.

"Your reader is on the bookcase," she said. "And there's a party for Ms. Rooney on Monday morning."

Then she marched out of the classroom.

Chapter 9

"Hurry," Emily said to Beast as they rushed across the schoolyard. "We have to get in there before Ms. Rooney comes."

"I hope she's not sick anymore," Beast said.

"Me too. Wait till you see this cake."

Richard pulled open the school door. "Don't drop it."

Emily held onto the box a little harder. "It's chocolate," she said, "because Alex likes chocolate."

"I like chocolate too," Beast said.

"One side has a whole lot of chocolate icing," Emily said. "That's because one side of the cake came out a little skinny." She tried to steady the box. "My mother says you can't tell."

"Who cares what it looks like?" Beast said.

"Me. I care," Emily said. "It's got tons of

gumdrops on it too. But don't worry. Just on one side."

"Here comes Dawn Bosco," Beast said. "The unicorn-stealer."

Emily looked over her shoulder.

Dawn was wearing a pink sweater just like Emily's green one.

Dawn was right. The pink one was prettier than the green.

"I told my father about the unicorn," Emily said.

"What did he say?"

"He said that Uni was a good friend, but he wasn't my good luck. He said that I should start over with Dawn. He said to be her friend. Maybe she was sad."

"What do you think?" Beast said.

Emily raised her shoulders. "Uni helped me run fast," she said. She smiled. "But I can fall asleep right away now. Even without him. My father says I'm growing up."

Emily poked her head around the classroom door.

Some of the kids were putting crepe paper on Ms. Rooney's desk.

Mrs. Paris was sitting on one of the desks. She was smiling.

"Is Ms. Rooney coming back?" Emily asked.

"Yes," Mrs. Paris said. "I called her this weekend. She said she didn't feel perfect. But I said she'd better come back. I said you were all lonesome for her."

"That's true," Jill said.

Emily put the cake carefully on her desk. Next to her Dawn was making a card for Ms. Rooney.

Emily remembered what her father had said. "That's a nice card," she told Dawn. She leaned over. "You don't spell Rooney with three *o*'s."

"I do," Dawn said.

"When Ms. Rooney comes," Matthew said, "we'll say 'Surprise!' " He batted a red balloon toward Beast.

71

"Maybe we won't have to do any work today," Alex said.

"Remember, Ms. Rooney doesn't feel perfect yet," Mrs. Paris said. "You'll have to be as good as gold."

Emily opened the box.

Dawn leaned over her shoulder. "That's a good cake," she said.

"I know," Emily said.

"It's a little lower on one side," Dawn said. "But I don't think anyone will notice."

Someone was coming down the hall.

Everyone ducked down.

Jim, the custodian, poked his head in the door.

"It's not Ms. Rooney," Matthew said.

"Someone's picking on the radiator," Jim said. "Someone's making a mess. I just painted that. Besides, it's dangerous to pick paint."

Emily put her head down. She made believe she was counting the gumdrops on her cake. She'd never touch that radiator again.

Dawn touched her shoulder. "He means you,"

she whispered. "But I won't tell. You found my book for me."

After a minute Jim went away.

Emily turned to Dawn. "I took your book. I was looking for—"

Dawn looked sad. "That's all right. I have to tell you something." She took a deep breath.

Emily looked at Dawn's face. She knew just what Dawn was going to say. She felt a big lump of happiness inside. She felt like making a fish face.

"I took your unicorn," Dawn said.

Emily nodded.

"And there's something else," Dawn said. "I didn't touch the tree."

Emily leaned over. "I don't—"

"The tree. The race on Tuesday. I cheated a little."

"That means I would have beaten you," Emily said. "Even without Uni."

"I'll give him back," Dawn said.

Emily smiled. "And you can show me how to do double Dutch jump rope. All right?"

"You'd be good at it," Dawn said.

Emily opened her mouth wide.

Then she shut it. Pop.

She began to laugh.

Dawn laughed too.

Just then more footsteps came down the hall.

This time it was Ms. Rooney.

Everyone yelled "Surprise!"

Even Mrs. Paris.

Ms. Rooney looked happy to be back. She smiled at everybody.

Emily couldn't wait to show her the cake. But then she was going to tell Dawn something. She was going to tell her that she didn't have a middle name. She was just plain old Emily Arrow.

But that was all right. She had just taken a look at Dawn's pencil. The initials were D.M.B.

Dawn's middle name wasn't Tiffanie.

It was probably something awful. Like Matilda.

Emily certainly hoped so.